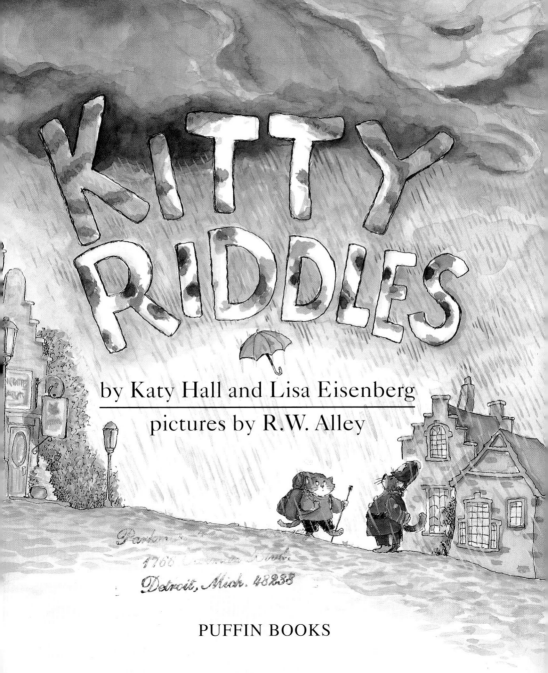

KITTY RIDDLES

by Katy Hall and Lisa Eisenberg

pictures by R.W. Alley

PUFFIN BOOKS

PUFFIN BOOKS
Published by the Penguin Group
Penguin Putnam Books for Young Readers, 345 Hudson Street, New York, New York 10014, U.S.A.
Penguin Books Ltd, 80 Strand, London WC2R ORL, England
Penguin Books Australia Ltd, Ringwood, Victoria, Australia
Penguin Books Canada Ltd, 10 Alcorn Avenue, Toronto, Ontario, Canada M4V 3B2
Penguin Books (N.Z.) Ltd, 182-190 Wairau Road, Auckland 10, New Zealand

Penguin Books Ltd, Registered Offices: Harmondsworth, Middlesex, England

First published in the United States of America by Dial Books for Young Readers,
a division of Penguin Putnam Inc., 2000
Published by Puffin Books, a division of Penguin Putnam Books for Young Readers., 2002

1 3 5 7 9 10 8 6 4 2

Text copyright © Kate McMullan and Lisa Eisenberg, 2000
Illustrations copyright © R.W. Alley, 2000

THE LIBRARY OF CONGRESS HAS CATALOGED THE DIAL EDITION AS FOLLOWS:
Hall, Katy
Kitty riddles/by Katy Hall and Lisa Eisenberg; pictures by R. W. Alley—1st ed.   p.   cm.
Summary: A collection of riddles about cats, including "Which famous kitty ruled Egypt?
Cleocatra!" and "How do kitties cut their grass? With a lawn meower!"
ISBN 0-8037-2116-1
1. Riddles, Juvenile. 2. Cats—Juvenile humor. [1. Cats—Wit and humor. 2. Riddles. 3. Jokes.]
I. Eisenberg, Lisa. II. Alley, R. W. (Robert W.), ill. III. Title.
PN6371.5.H3485   2000   818'.5402—dc21   97-37438   CIP   AC

Puffin Books ISBN 0-14-230082-9
Puffin® and Easy-to-Read® are registered trademarks of Penguin Putnam Inc.
Printed in Hong Kong
Designed by Sara Reynolds

The full-color artwork was prepared using ink and watercolor.

Reading Level 2.6

CAT CITY CHRONICLE

Dedicated to Groucho, the best kitty in the world
　　　　　—K.H.

In memory of Puck
　　　　　—L.E.

To Tanya and Fluffy
　　　　　—R.W.A.

What do you call a kitty with a
can of tuna?

Purr-fectly happy!

Why did the baby cat carry
around a box of Band-Aids?

She wanted to be a first-aid kit!

What do kitties like to put on their mouse-burgers?

Cats-up!

What did the kitty say when
the mouse got away?

Oh, rats!

What kind of kitties are the best bowlers?

Alley cats!

Which famous kitty ruled
Egypt?

Cleocatra!

How do kitties cut their grass?

With a lawn meower!

What kind of kitty has eight
legs?

An octo-puss!

Why do kitties sing so well?

They're very mewsical.

Where do kitties find out
what's happening?

From the *Daily Mews*!

What mountains do kitties love?

The Catskills!

Do kitties like to shop in stores?

No, they prefer catalogs!

What do kitties eat for
breakfast?

Mice Krispies and Puffed Mice!

What ancient land had the
happiest cats?

Purr-sia!

What do you call a kitty that eats a duck?

A duck-filled fatty puss!

What do you call a fight
between two kitties?

A cat-astrophe!

Why did the kitty let the genie out of the bottle?

She was hoping she'd be granted three fishes!

What's little and soft and says,
"Beow! Beow!"

A kitty with a cold!

Can your pet kitty ever learn to like your pet bird?

Yes, especially with barbecue sauce!

What's a kitty's favorite color?

Purrple!

How should you pet an angry, wet kitty?

From fur, fur away!

How do cats find out they're going to be parents?

They get a litter!

Who's the most famous cat
from the Wild West?

Kitty Carson!

What do kitties do on the
Fourth of July?

They march in big purr-ades.

What game do kitties play at birthday parties?

Mewsical chairs!

Why did the kitty move to a
new neighborhood?

Because the old one was
going to the dogs!

What do you get if you cross a
kitty and a snapping turtle?

Cat nip!

What kind of kitty wears sunglasses and a raincoat and says, "Bow wow"?

An impawstor.

What do you call a kitty with pigtails?

A braidy-cat!

Is it really unlucky to see a
black cat?

Only if you're a mouse!

What prize did the movie star
kitty hope to win?

The A-cat-emy Award!

What are kitty's favorite
subjects in school?

Mewsic, Hisstory, Fureign
Languages, and Fishing.

What do you get if you cross a
cat with a laughing hyena?

A giggle puss.

When it rains cats and dogs,
what do kitties avoid?

Poodles.